Orange Zen

The birth of the Pumpking

Introduction

I don't know where to start, how do I even begin to explain how I ended up in the situation i'm in? Was it fate? Was I always destined to end up in a fight for my life against a crime lord while trying to rescue a Dove from a Synexus bounty hunter? Fuck no! But if this is fate, all I have to say is two words, Fuck destiny. My name is Sicarius Knight, before my life went to hell I was just an average guy living with my girlfriend and working as a computer programmer for one of the biggest tech companies in Skyguard City, I think back now about how peaceful things were, but if I'm honest, even in the midst of the craziness I have somehow got myself into, I wouldn't change a thing.

Episode 1

My life came crashing down around me three months ago, the woman I was gonna propose to dumped me in a text, a fucking text! Oddly enough she said it was cause she felt we were moving too slow in our relationship and basically she felt I wasn't ready to get married, oh the irony. Yeah I know what

you're thinking, why
didn't I just tell her I
was going to propose,
hell I even had the
ring as proof, but you
see right before I got
that text my mom
called to inform me
that my father lost his
fight against cancer, I
mean talk about
terrible timing. In the
few brief seconds I
had to process the loss
of my father, I just

didn't have any time to give a fuck about someone who would dump someone in a fucking text! If that wasn't bad enough a week later I received notice that my employment was terminated, now I admit even though I was going through shit I should have filled my boss in on my fathers passing instead of just not showing up for work, but hindsight is twenty twenty, and during that time I didn't care about anything, or so I thought. Numb to the world around me I found myself driving nowhere in no rush to get there, which I guess more than pissed off a few other drivers. Through all

the noise of honking
and profanity being
hurled my way, I
somehow manage to
maintain a speed that
looking back now
matched how I was
feeling, that is until I
pulled up to a red
light alongside what
felt like was my
complete opposite, a
guy who had
everything, driving
with the top down on

his red VX Hell
Hound, beautiful girl
in the passenger seat,
I hated this guy! Yet
didn't know him, as if
in that moment I just
needed someone to
blame, someone to
hate, for everything
wrong in my life, it
felt like even his car
was mocking mine,
bright red Valkyrie X
bullshit Hell Hound,
who even drives a

Valkyrie except rich showoff assholes "what a dick" is all I could think while I gripped my steering wheel hard enough to snap it, foot pressing down on the brake pad with the entirety of my body weight, I was pissed off to say the least, my blood felt like fire and when the light turned green, this random guy

whom I will never
know, who never did
a single thing to me,
inadvertently became
the last straw that set
me on the path I'm
on today. What was it
you ask? What did
this guy do that was
so horrible? He
simply drove away,
but in my delusional
mind he was
challenging me,
taunting me, hell he

was daring me to pass him, after all he had everything and in that moment he was telling me he owned the road as well, his engine roared like a lion warning inferior males to stay far away from his territory, and I refused to be seen as inferior, I needed to pass him, I couldn't lose the last thing I had in this world, which was, my right to travel? I don't know I was crazy at the time, but I knew there was a reason I couldn't lose to him, not during that time, I don't think I could've handled more loss. So I took a breathe, looked at the green light and then ahead at the red Valkyrie asshole speeding away, I took my foot off the brake placed it on the gas and never looked back. Theres no way to really capture in words what happened next, its one of those you gotta experience it for yourself moments, although I don't recommend it, the best way I could try and describe it, is as a blur of emotion, colors, sounds and light. Like living in the painting of an artist with a twistedly frightening yet colorful imagination. Speeding at over a hundred miles an hour I felt like any moment I was going to die, and that I was too fast to even try and slow down. Colors flooded my line of sight from the lights outside my car

widows, streaming in
like some sort of
rainbow light circus, it
was beautifully
frightening, these
neon lights from store
fronts and street
lamps and car head
lights, consumed my
full attention and
contrasted gorgeously
against the pitch black
night sky, in fact I
found myself looking
up at the sky simply to

avoid being sucked into the blinding light burning through my windshield. At well over a hundred miles an hour for a brief moment I wasn't watching the road, the initial fear of death faded and anger poured back into me, I realized I wasn't driving to end up dead in some car crash, I was in a race against some red Valkyrie driving jackass, my attention quickly returned to the road, my eyes began to adjust to the speed in which lights came in and out of my line of sight, my high beams raced ahead of my car like blood hounds searching for my pray, car after car I passed swerving in and out of lanes, I felt like a Nag, suddenly my mind was clear no more pain no more grief, I didn't have time to think about my life because any hesitation while at the speed I was at could lead to my death, and somehow that brought me peace, that all I had to worry about was driving. It didn't take long to realize that I probably already passed the Valkyrie considering I had been speeding and running more than a few red lights and never caught up to the guy, but at that point I had bigger problems, I had been so focused on the lights in front of me I neglected the lights behind me, red and blue lights to be exact.

Like lightning surging
through my body, a
sense of exhilaration
took hold of me. I was
pulled out of the river
of light I was lost in
and snapped back
into reality, fully alert
I had one goal, not
getting arrested.
Three squad cars
raced behind me,
sirens screaming at
me to stop, while my
engines roar yelled

back "never you assholes". Every hair on my body was standing on end as I raced through the city to escape the SGPD, with the squad cars closing in on me fast with no turns in sight and a freight train seconds from blocking my path to freedom my options were clear, keep going and risk ending up a stain on the front of the freight train, or stop and be arrested? Hell I decided on option three, go faster then my orange antique Skypiercer was ever meant to go, which was about as fast as these old classic muscle cars used to go back when they owned the road, and hopefully, not end up dead under a freight train. With my plan being the only thing in mind I stepped down hard on the gas and flew towards what seemed like certain death. As the railway gate came down I just barely squeezed through before the train raced by closing off the path between me and the cops, with no time to celebrate I quickly kept going taking back streets and of course following traffic laws and speed limits until I finally made it home. I was amped, in one night I had faced death multiple times, avoided arrest and broke the law, even safe at home I didn't know if the cops would kick down my door with a warrant

after tracing my
license plate, and yet I
couldn't stop
laughing, I was so
overjoyed to be alive
and free, that night I
didn't get a wink of
sleep I stayed up the
whole time waiting for
the cops to come but
they never did,
somehow I was really
home free, until I
heard pounding on
my door and quickly

started to panic again, but at that point there was nowhere left to run, so I walked towards the pounding which felt like sacrificial drums ready to accept my fate. The walk to my front door felt like an eternity, for some odd reason I kept thinking to myself "what if I go to prison? Will I ever be able to have ice cream again" these thoughts were really plaguing me ya know? Its funny the thoughts that go through your head in times of crisis, I began to open the door expecting to see a full S.W.A.T team in front of my house, but instead, in barged a strange girl whom I've never met. At first I was shocked and in awe of this beautiful

girl walking around
my living room
looking around as if
she owned the place, I
was speechless,
nothing could come
to mind to say, but a
weight was lifted off
my shoulders knowing
it wasn't the cops at
my door. Finally after
walking around
looking through my
family photos and
other things I had

laying around the strange girl spoke.

Strange girl: "Hey, hows it going?"

Sicarius Knight: "Pretty good I guess"

Yup, "pretty good I guess" was the first thing that popped into my mind, not who are you? Or why are you here? "Just pretty good I guess" as if it was totally normal for strangers to walk up into my house. To say this girl was beautiful doesn't do her justice, her hair flowed like silk waves and was as black as the night sky, she had the deepest most adorable dimples you could see even when she wasn't smiling, her skin was smooth and tan like the sand of a beach during a sunset, and her body, her body personified perfection, she was a Naggess.

Strange girl: "Do you know why I'm here?"

Do I know why your here? Hell no, if you hadn't noticed I don't know you, I said in my mind while staring at her with a puzzled look on my face.

Sicarius Knight: "Um, I don't know really"

Strange girl: "You don't know, I doubt that, why don't you take a guess"

Now I was seriously confused considering this girl seemed to think I should know why she was at my home, but I decided to think back, maybe I saw or met her somewhere before, however I kept drawing a blank.

Sicarius Knight: "I honestly don't know, I don't think we ever met before"

Strange girl: "We haven't, but that little pumpkin of yours sure did meet my cherry bomber"
What the fuck was this girl talking about?

Sicarius Knight: "Little pumpkin? I

don't know what you mean"

Strange girl: "I figured you hadn't named him yet, guess I was right, your just some noob"
I was lost, and that is a feeling I hate, and this girls condescending attitude wasn't helping.

Sicarius Knight:
"Why don't we start
over, I'm Sicarius,
whats your name?
And why are you
here?"

Strange girl: "My
name's Alexis Rouge,
but everyone knows
me as The Red Deva,
as for why I'm here,
thats a riot, last night
on my way to a burn

out you decided to call me out for an unscheduled burn"

Everything she was saying sounded foreign to me, however I started to look past her beauty and noticed a few telling signs that I was missing, for one she had tattoos, they were small but not the common girly tattoos most girls get, these seemed gang affiliated, secondly she was wearing what looked like a sports biker jacket, red leather with different custom logos including one cherry bomber patch and a Red Deva name patch, it was clear this girl was in some kind of gang, but where could I have crossed paths with her?

Sicarius Knight: "Maybe you got the wrong guy, I don't remember calling you out and I don't even know what a burn out is"

Alexis Rouge: "You mean to tell me I got

blazed, not by a noob, but by a civilian? A common pedestrian?"

Sicarius knight: "Maybe? I can't tell you one way or the other because I don't recognize you"

Alexis Rouge: "Take a look out the fucking window"

Fear reclaimed me, what was outside my window? Did she bring her gang with her? So many questions raced through my mind but the mystery of who she was intrigued me the most, so I walked to my window peeked through the blinds and thats when I knew exactly who she was.

Sicarius Knight:
"Your the red
Valkyrie asshole"

Yeah I realized how
that sounded after I
blurted it out, but in
the moment it just
slipped.

Alexis Rouge: "Red Valkyrie asshole? So you do remember my Cherry bomber?"

Sicarius Knight: "So little pumpkin?"

Alexis Rouge: "Thats right, its that little hunk of junk you call a blazer"

Sicarius Knight: "Look I don't know what a blazer or burn out is but lets not forget that little hunk of junk sure blazed you and that can of tomato sauce you call a sports car"

At that moment I knew I was losing my mind, what the hell was I saying? And why was I arguing with this girl? But most of all why was she a girl? I could have sworn it was a guy who pulled up beside me. I started to think back and thats when it hit me, the red Valkyrie drove up with tinted windows

and the top up, then I
must have imagined
what I wanted to
because I was upset,
simple case of hysteria
please don't judge me.

Alexis Rouge: "Can
of tomato sauce? My
Cherry Bomber is the

greatest blazer ever built, her shell might be a red Valkyrie but underneath her hood she's fully customized, for street racing"

Sicarius Knight: "So your a street racer"

Alexis Rouge: "Ah duh jackass, haven't you been listening"

Sicarius Knight: "Not really since I left you in my dust slowpoke"

Alexis Rouge: "Now you've crossed the fucking line, I'm the complete fucking opposite of slow, get in that pumpkin and lets race"

Sicarius Knight: "You couldn't keep up with Lil Pumpkin on his worst day maybe I should use a pedal bike"
Alexis Rouge: "Cocky, I like that, just know last night was a fluke, I wasn't prepared to go racing through traffic

endangering innocent
peoples lives for some
psychotic edge rider"

Sicarius Knight:
"Psychotic?"
Alexis Rouge: "Yeah,
thats what you edge
riders are, just a
bunch of thrill seeking
psychos"

Her words cut deep, I
didn't even stop to
think of all the lives I
put in danger during
my temper tantrum
on the road, how
could I be so reckless?
Why didn't I realize

the stakes? I could
only stand there
unable to look her in
the eyes due to the
overwhelming sense
of guilt I felt.
Alexis Rouge: "What?
Nothing to say for
yourself?"

I took a moment to
collect myself, after a

deep breath I decided to speak from the heart.

Sicarius Knight: "Listen, I don't know what an edge rider or anything else you've been talking about is, but I do know what I did last night was wrong, I can't even imagine being responsible for

causing someones
injury or worse
someones death, I
have no excuse for
what I did, to be
honest I guess
everything that sucks
in my life just started
to pile up and I
snapped, sadly even
though I regret every
moment, I'm
ashamed to admit
that last night I felt

more at peace then I felt in a long time."

Alexis Rouge: "Then how about an official race?"

Sicarius Knight: "Wait what?"

Alexis Rouge: "Racing is about more than just proving how fast you are, its about freedom and getting closer to who you truly are by staring death in the eyes, you saw it didn't you?"

Sicarius Knight: "Saw what?"

Alexis Rouge: "The veil, between life and death, its the only way a noob could have out raced me"

Sicarius Knight: "I don't know what I saw, but I know what I felt"

Alexis Rouge: "So it's settled, theres a race scheduled in a few days you're gonna need practice"

Sicarius Knight: "Wait what?

Alexis Rouge: "You have to race, now that you got a taste of it you won't be able to resist trust me, but the choice is yours meet me at The Blue Walrus its a bar on route 98, if you change your mind that is"

As she left a part of
me wanted to chase
after her, I knew what
she said was true, I
could feel it, now that
I have experienced
the adrenaline rush of
racing I couldn't just
go back to normal like
nothing happened,
my eyes were open.
I would love to say I
thought about her
offer but in reality I
didn't need to, I had

nothing to lose, so I grabbed my keys hopped into my car and headed to The Blue Walrus. As I was heading to the bar so many ideas popped into my head of what it would be like, I envisioned drugs, guns, tatted up bikers and an all around unsavory atmosphere which made me more then a little nervous, but when I got there I couldn't believe my eyes, the big bad Blue Walrus was a juice bar I couldn't help but smile knowing that I was safe, I mean how dangerous could things get as people were buying smoothies and cold pressed drinks? As I pulled into the parking lot I saw Alexis and her Cherry

Bomber she was parked near three other cars, a blue off road GXA 77 also known as the great ark for its size and immaculate build design, the sheer sight of that behemoth made all other cars seem like mere toys in comparison, the next was a green 1975 Drift Demon manufactured during

the hight of early
Tawnyo city drift
races and outlawed in
1980 for being too
dangerous to handle,
the shape almost
made it look like a
living creature, its
belly so low to the
ground a razor could
only barely squeeze
underneath it and its
wheels were twice the
size of normal tires
which gave off the

appearance that this creature could pounce at any moment, and last but certainly not least, a black Nag Slayer, clearly a replica but still there are only 14 replicas of the Nag Slayer in existence all manufactured by Cyberus one of the top weapons manufactures in the world who's founder

Niguel Cyberus went missing after being diagnosed with and incurable health condition and allegedly went mad vowing to design a car fast enough to out run not only death but Nazeerah himself, legend has it he created the Nag Slayer and was able to escape Nazeerahs Will, all anyone really knows is both Niguel Cyberus and the original Nag Slayer haven't been seen in years, this car certainly lived up to the hype, its frame was otherworldly an futuristic, it looked more like a cross between a fighter jet and a Nagxhip than a car, and the paint job just made it that much more awe inspiring a deep rich dark metallic paint coated its entirety, it felt as if staring for to long would plunge me into a world of darkness. These guys were way out of my league, it was easy to see they were a crew, each had a racing jacket that matched the color of their car, I admit I was intimidated, these cars weren't just symbols of their wealth and status, they were symbols that these guys were pros. Seeing Alexis with these three guys gave me a new found respect for her, I couldn't help but think to myself how good she must be to be the only girl in their crew, I started to think maybe I should quit while I was ahead and just leave before she spots me, and as soon as that thought escaped my head, she spotted me. I thought about just driving away as she motioned to me to come over, but I was already there so I decided to see it through, I pulled up and parked alongside the black Nag Slayer, our cars

were like night and
day, and so were we,
these guys looked like
runway models, I
mean I'm no slouch I
hit the gym and I
train in self defense
not to mention more
then a few women
have told me I'm
handsome but I felt
like me and these guys
were from totally
different worlds, I
didn't have much

time to think before
they started to
introduce themselves,
the first was Joshua
Stone aka Baby Jekon
the rider of the GxA
77 known as Fortress,
the second was Derick
West aka
Code Breaker the
rider of the Drift
Demon known as
Dart Frog, the last
was Kevin Steel aka
The Xkaredio, the

rider of the Nag Slayer known as Death Scythe, they all seemed so sure of themselves, so confident in who they are, but what about me? Who was I ?

Alexis Rouge; "So who are you?"

It's like she read my mind and knew I

wasn't sure of who I was anymore, after all the old me seemed so far away, but who was I now?

Joshua Stone; "Maybe that question is a bit advance for a beginner, have you at least named your car?"

Alexis Rouge; "Not exactly, he can thank me for that"

Joshua Stone; "You can't name someone else's blazer, a cars name comes from its riders soul"

They argued backed and forth about choosing a name for a car, before long all four of them were in on the debate, lost in thought I blocked out the noise, everything became silent all I could think about was what my cars name is, I turned to look at my car and I knew one hundred percent.

Sicarius Knight; "Lil Pumpkin, my cars name is Lil Pumpkin"

Alexis Rouge; "Wow you shortened little to lil, very creative"

Joshua Stone; "Dude you can't use a name someone else came up with"

Sicarius Knight; "I'm not, Lil Pumpkin is just his start not his end, it's the name that will begin our journey until he tells me his true name and I find mine"

Alexis Rouge; "Beautifully explained, now that that's out the way, lets get this show on the road shall we?"

Kevin Steel; "First things first, is it true you lost to this dude

in what appears to be
a junk yard car?"
Joshua Stone; "His
name's Lil Pumpkin,
show some respect"

Derick West; "It
doesn't matter if he
won or not it wasn't
officially a race"

Sicarius Knight;
"You're right, it
wasn't, so to answer

you're question, no she didn't lose to me" Alexis Rouge; "First off, I can speak for myself, secondly, I lost, I chose to chase after a random edge rider only to see if I could pass him out of pride, and yet I never could"

Kevin Steel; "Well then, this guy must be

good, can't wait to see for myself"

Joshua Stone; "You beat The Red Deva? Guys what if he can beat?"

Kevin Steel; "Impossible, there's only one person who will beat him and that's me"

Sicarius Knight; "Beat who?'"

Derick West; "The Red Krowlock"

Alexis Rouge; "Enough, and besides the only person that can beat him is me, after I beat this chump and reclaim my undefeated record"

Whoever this Red Krowlock was he clearly was their objective, their faces each told a different story, Joshua seemed to idolize The Red Krowlock or at the very least respect him, Derick seemed afraid of just the thought of him, Kevin's face was filled with hatred, and Alexis seemed saddened, who was this guy? Why did he cause them to feel so many different emotions? I wanted to ask, but knew that none of them wanted to answer questions about him, not at that moment anyway. After a few drinks we all left The Blue Walrus and headed back to Joshua's house for what they said would be training, instead we just goofed off, within hours we had a miniature party going on, snacks, music, I was having more fun then I had in a long time and within no time I felt like I had known these idiots my whole life, Kevin was being a debbie downer, just brooding in the corner alone, but even that felt

natural to me as if I
always knew him and
it was just Kevin
being Kevin, before
long night fell and the
mood changed,
everyones once goofy
personalities turned
serious and an
overwhelming sense
of excitement was in
the air, even Kevin
who was once sulking
had a slight smirk on
his face, without

anyone saying a word to me I knew what time it was, I felt the urge just as strongly as they did, and thats when I knew, this was my pack, I was one of them, and it was time to race. The race was set, it was a private match between the five of us clearly designed to test our metal and decide our rank, the rules were

simple to race up a
mountain road till we
reach the top then
turn around and
make it down first
And for me this was
even more than just
about rank or to
prove my skill, I knew
this race would be
when I discover my
name. The race was
set for midnight, our
cars lined up side by
side at the bottom of

the mountain, engines roaring at each other as if our cars were talking trash to one another, my eyes were focused on the time, one minute to midnight, one minute until I left my past behind me and become a new person, in that minute I felt so many different emotions, from fear and anxiety, to excitement and anticipation, and then, it was midnight. Within seconds a cloud of smoke engulfed our cars, created by a synchronized burnout, our vision cut off from the road ahead, all anyone could see was the illuminated smoke as our high beams cut a path through nothingness. I couldn't hesitate, I had to be first, blindly I rushed into the nothingness ahead racing towards my destiny. Coming out the other side finally free of the smoke the light of my high beams slid across the slick black road guiding my path forward, a stark contrast to the pitch black darkness I saw behind me in my rearview mirror, where was everybody? Did I create that much distance out the gate that they still hadn't caught up? I was starting to think I had the race won before it even started, whipping around corners clawing my way up the side of the mountain, before long

I made it to the top only to discover that I was the last to make it, I looked at the time and only ten minutes had past, how could they have made it here before me in under ten minutes? Their cars were lined up in front of me as if they were waiting and as I sat in my car facing them none of them made a move, wasn't the race still on? Were they taunting me? Daring me to try and make it down before them and even giving me a head start. It didn't matter, I had to win, quickly I begun to turn around, but before I could I was once again engulfed in smoke as their wheels scorched the earth and they raced past me, I felt defeated but only for a moment, I knew there wasn't enough time for self doubt, I raced on following the trail of lights their cars created in front of me. They were all so incredible, the way they moved and their speed, I knew I couldn't match them, but there was one flaw, one singular pattern they all followed, watching them I noticed they would hug the side of the mountain while on a straight path in order to avoid turning wide during a turn, I knew this was to avoid crashing and falling off the side of the mountain, but for me it was something I could exploit, and it was my only option.

The only way my plan would work is if I accomplished three task, they didn't see me coming, I maintained my speed, and I was willing to die to win, I thought about my father, who was a decorated fighter pilot in the air force, he would always tell me that a mans true strength is his willingness to die

for the people he loves
and what he believes
in, he also told me
what sets those who
are considered great
apart from those who
are average is their
willingness to do what
no one else is willing
to do. The people I
love? My mother is all
that came to mind, I
mean I had
acquaintances but
these guys I just met

feel more like friends then anyone else in my life, and as for my mom she always told me follow my heart. What do I believe in? At the moment, just this, this urge I have inside to be the fastest, to be the best. It was decided, there was no way I was gonna lose this race. I switched off all the lights on my car, I

needed to be a ghost,
I then pressed down
on the gas with all my
might, I only needed
to stay close enough
to each car so I could
pass them on their
outside during a turn.
First was Dart Frog,
Lil Pumpkin snuck up
behind him trailing
his every move until
the moment of truth,
a sharp turn that
would either be the

death of me or get me one step closer to winning. A turn that took less then a second felt like forever, all I could sense was a quiet calm, I could feel Lil Pumpkins wheels struggling to stay planted on the road, I instinctively started switching back and forth between my break and gas pedal

as my tires screeched
and my taillights just
barely scraped the
railing, gripping my
steering wheel for
dear life, my heart
racing at a million
miles per second, I felt
a strange peace, a sort
of zen like experience,
before I knew it I was
out in front of Derick,
however it was too
little too late, even
trying to gun it, that

was the last turn and it was a straight shot to the bottom. I lost, but it felt like a win, like I was a new person, when we all made it down to the bottom we all began to celebrate, everyone seemed genuinely happy to just be alive, thats when I finally realized what Alexis meant by the veil between life and death, racing meant risking death and the reward was surviving, it gave them a reason for living by reminding them how precious life truly is, and now I felt it, its hard to sulk and feel self pity after a near death experience, I was finally alive once again, my ex was the past, my father would live on forever in his teachings he bestowed on me, my job was to live fast and have a blast doing it.

Alexis Rouge; "But what's your name?"

Once again with this mind reading.

Alexis Rouge; "After all you beat Derick, and came in fourth place, with moves like yours you gotta have a name"

Joshua Stone; "It's true, we never expected you to beat one of us we just wanted to test out your skill level, but

turns out you're a
natural"

Kevin Steel; "They're
right even I can admit
you're better than I
expected or maybe
Derick is just worse
than expected either

way you earned my respect"

Derick West; "Worse than expected? Coming from a guy who always comes in second place to Alexis"

Kevin Steel; "Oh yeah? And you always come in fourth place, but I guess we got a new fourth which makes you officially our fifth place member"

Alexis Rouge;
"Enough, now tell us
who you are? And
what's your name?"

Sicarius Knight; "I'm
the rider of Lil
Pumpkin, and my
name? Is Orange
Zen"

To be continued…

www.ingramcontent.com/pod-product-compliance
Lightning Source LLC
Chambersburg PA
CBHW050412030726
47503CB00006B/2157